Oliver Moon and the Spell-Off

Sue Mongredien

Illustrated by

Jan McCafferty

USBORNE

For Harry Graves, with lots of love

First published in 2007 by Usborne Publishing Ltd., Usborne House,
83-85 Saffron Hill, London EC1N 8RT, England. www.usborne.com

A CIP catalogue record for this book is available from
the British Library.

UK ISBN 9780746077948 First published in America in 2011 AE.

American ISBN 9780794530938 JFM MJJASOND/11 01314/1

Printed in Dongguan, Guangdong, China.

Contents

Chapter One

The Moon family was having breakfast
one morning when they heard a
familiar rattle from the front door.
"Mail-monster coming!" the letterbox
announced. "Late as usual, I see – what
a surprise! Oof!"

There was a thud, as the mail fell onto
the doormat.

"No need to be so rough!" Oliver heard the letterbox scold the mail-monster. "Just because you're in a hurry! Shouldn't have overslept again, should you?"

Mr. Moon, Oliver's dad, frowned. "That letterbox is getting a little too fresh," he commented, with a slurp of his cockroach coffee. "Must get around to putting a magic muffler on it."

The Witch Baby, Oliver's sister, was straining to get out of her high chair. "Down!" she was saying excitedly. "Me see monster!"

Mrs. Moon gave her a smile. "Not today, pickle," she replied. "He's already gone. Eat up your beetle flakes, there's a good girl."

Oliver finished his batwing toast, and got up from the table to collect the mail.

"Not much this morning," the letterbox told him, swinging open as it spoke. "A letter for your dad there, and your mom's *Witch Weekly* magazine. Oh, and some bills, too, I'm afraid." It shut again with a loud snap.

"Thanks," Oliver said politely, gathering up the pile and taking it to his parents. It was a Saturday morning, so there was no rush for him to go to Magic School, or for his dad to fly off to work. He sat back down at the table, and spread some jellyfish jelly on a second slice of toast.

"Ooh," his mom said, flicking through her new magazine. "*Green* capes are in this season. Nice… And, ooh, those pumpkin fritters look yummy, I wonder how you—"

She was interrupted by Mr. Moon jumping to his feet with a shout. "I've got it!" he yelled, waving his letter in the air. "I've actually gotten it!"

"Got what?" Oliver asked with interest.

His dad had jumped up so quickly, he'd knocked the plate of batwing toast off the table.

"Fleas," giggled his sister. "Daddy got fleas!"

Mrs. Moon dragged her eyes away from "101 New Pumpkin Recipes" to

look at her husband. "What's that, dear?" she asked distractedly.

"The job!" Mr. Moon cried, a grin on his face. He flung his arms wide, elbowing a vase of stinkweed off the shelf behind him in all the excitement. "I got the job!"

"Really?" Oliver's mom jumped to her feet, fritters forgotten. "Let's see!"

"What job?" Oliver asked. "What are you talking about? You're leaving ValuStix?"

"I certainly am," said Mr. Moon, passing the letter to his wife with a flourish. "I've been offered a job, Oliver. At your school!"

Oliver's eyes boggled at the news. His dad working at Magic School? Oliver knew Mr. Moon had never really enjoyed his job as a broomstick salesman, but he'd had no idea he was thinking of leaving. "But... But..." he stammered, trying to take it in. "But what are you going to be doing at Magic School? You're not... You're not going to be a *teacher*, are you?"

Oliver crossed his fingers behind his back. He really didn't want his dad to be one of his teachers. It would be so embarrassing!

"Not a teacher, no," his dad replied. "I'm the new Potions assistant. I'll be helping out with the experiments, that sort of thing."

"Well done, darling!" Mrs. Moon cried, throwing her arms around her husband's neck. "That's so exciting!"

Oliver stared at his beaming parents. He couldn't help feeling surprised. The current Potions assistant at school, Mr. Newt, was one of the smartest people Oliver had ever met. Whereas Mr. Moon... Well. He was just...*Dad.*

"Um…Dad," Oliver said, choosing his words carefully, "do you actually *know* much about potions?"

Mr. Moon shrugged. "Well, I *used* to," he said breezily. "Quite a few years ago, anyway. Won the school prize for Potions, back when I was a boy." He smiled. He poured himself another cup of cockroach coffee, splashing some on the tablecloth by mistake.

"And it can't be any harder than trying to sell a load of crummy broomsticks every day! What could possibly go wrong?"

Oliver finished his breakfast thoughtfully. He didn't want to pour cold water on his dad's excitement, but Mr. Newt was always telling them that you needed a steady hand in the Potions room, especially when you were using live ingredients. And Mr. Moon was rather... well, clumsy at times. *And* there was all sorts of new Potions equipment at school that his dad would have to learn to use.

Oliver couldn't help feeling slightly nervous at the thought of his dad working in the Potions room. In his opinion, there were *lots* of things that could go wrong!

Chapter
Two

A week or so later, Oliver and Jake were
joined on their usual morning walk to
school by Mr. Moon. It was his first day
in his new job. "Isn't this exciting?" he
kept saying. "Isn't this fun? All of us
going to school together, eh?"

Oliver looked over at Jake, who was
bouncing his skull football in silence.

Usually on a Monday morning, Oliver and Jake chatted nonstop about Saturday's big wizardball match, or what they'd been up to over the weekend. It wasn't really the same with Mr. Moon walking between them.

"Um…yeah, Dad," Oliver replied after a moment. They'd reached the school gates now, and he stopped. "Dad — the staff room is that way. Go and ask for Mrs. MacLizard. She'll help you. Good luck and…be careful!"

Oliver watched his dad go, and crossed his fingers. He hoped everything would go all right in the Potions room. He'd been testing his dad on his ingredients last night, and was a little worried that Mr. Moon seemed to have forgotten almost *everything* about potions. He kept getting frogspawn and toadspawn mixed up, he couldn't tell the cat claws from the bat claws, and he'd knocked over a whole box of red ants by mistake.

"Steady hand, Dad!" Oliver had reminded him, wincing as the Witch Baby tried to eat a handful of wriggling ants.

Oliver crossed the fingers on his other hand too, as he saw his dad walk into the school. Oh, he so hoped Dad would be okay!

Later on, Oliver's class had their Potions lesson as usual. It was strange, walking into the Potions room without cheerful

Mr. Newt greeting everybody by name. Instead, there was Mr. Moon at the back of the room. Oliver bit his lip as he saw that his dad was trying to wrestle a long, hissing snake back into its glass box. Mr. Moon already had a strange purple stain down the front of his overalls, Oliver noticed in alarm.

"Ahh, our new assistant," Oliver's teacher, Mr. Goosepimple, said politely. "Class — this is Mr. Moon. Is…er…is everything all right there, Mr. Moon?"

The class watched with interest as Mr. Moon squeezed the squirming snake safely back into its box and locked the lid. Then he turned to face the class, red-faced and panting slightly, but trying to smile. "Hi, everyone," he said.

In the front row, Lucy Lizardlegs was giggling and nudging her best friend Carly Catstail.

Oliver wondered why – until he noticed the death beetles crawling out of Mr. Moon's front pocket. What were they doing *there*?

"What's that in your dad's ear?" Jake hissed, elbowing Oliver.

Oliver hardly dared look. But when he did… Oh, no. There was a weevilworm coiled around Mr. Moon's ear lobe. Had his dad forgotten that  weevilworms gave nasty little nips?

"Okay, let's get on with our lesson," Mr. Goosepimple said, with another rather apprehensive glance at Mr. Moon. "We're going to make a Slime potion today. I believe Mr. Moon has already prepared the ingredients for this, so—"

CREEEEAK!

Mr. Goosepimple stopped speaking

as the classroom door opened. Mrs.
MacLizard, the head teacher, walked into
the room, with her arm around a boy
Oliver didn't recognize. The boy looked
to be around Oliver's age, and was
staring around the room with a smirk on
his face.

"Sorry to interrupt," Mrs. MacLizard said, "but I'd like to introduce you all to Casper, my nephew. He's staying with me for a few weeks, so I thought he should join your class for that time. Everybody, this is Casper. He's sure to teach you all a thing or two, he's *very* bright!"

She ruffled Casper's hair fondly, and he stared down his nose at Oliver's classmates.

"Now, Casper, this is the Potions room," Mrs. MacLizard went on. "Casper is an *expert* on Potions, by the way. So what are we making in here, then?"

A sudden yelp came from Mr. Moon's direction. Everyone turned to see him clamping a hand to his ear, trying to wrench off the weevilworm that had sunk its fangs into him.

Lucy and Carly giggled again. Some of the boys snickered. And Bully Bogeywort, Oliver's worst enemy at school, laughed out loud.

"Everything all right, Mr. Moon?" Mrs. MacLizard asked.

"Yes…fine…" grunted Mr. Moon, wincing in pain. The weevilworm finally came away with a tearing sound, and Mr. Moon shook it off his fingers and onto the floor. "Sorry – please continue. Don't mind me!"

There was a small pause, then Mr. Goosepimple turned back to the head teacher. "We're practicing our Slime potions," he told her. "Perhaps you'd like to stay and watch while we put one together? Mr. Moon – if you'd be so kind as to pass out the ingredients?"

Mr. Moon looked rather nervous under the beady eyes of Mrs. MacLizard, Oliver thought. He watched his dad hurry around with the potion ingredients, handing them to each student.

"Thank you, Mr. Moon," said Mr. Goosepimple. "Now, we made this potion last Tuesday, didn't we? So let's see how well you remember it. Pippi, would you demonstrate it for us, please?"

Pippi Prowlcat beamed and got to her feet. Oliver could tell she was proud at the chance to show off her cleverness with the head teacher in the room. "First, I'll put in a spoonful of spider legs," she said loudly, measuring some and pouring them into her potion beaker.

"And then a cupful of snake spit…"

She carefully measured out the snake spit – and Oliver saw his dad turn pale. "Snake spit?" Mr. Moon muttered, as Pippi poured it into the beaker. "But that's not… Oh, no. No! WAIT!" But it

was too late. There was an almighty
BOOM! from the beaker, a scream from
Pippi…and then clouds of billowing
black smoke engulfed the whole
classroom.

Chapter Three

"Sorry, everybody!" Mr. Moon shouted through the smoke. "I thought it was supposed to be *snail slime*!"

Oliver and the rest of the class began coughing and spluttering in the thick smoke. Oliver's eyes stung and he tried to fan it away from his face. He couldn't see a thing!

"Pippi, are you all right?" Mr.
Goosepimple called anxiously. "Pippi?"

Mrs. MacLizard's voice rang out before
Pippi could reply. "Vanish, smoke! This is
no joke!" she chanted. Oliver heard her
wand swishing through the air and then,
seconds later, the smoke cleared.

Oliver blinked and rubbed his eyes as the last few black curls of smoke vanished into the end of Mrs. MacLizard's wand. "There," she said, gazing around. "Is everyone okay?"

Pippi Prowlcat had soot all over her face and a singed braid. "What…what happened?" she asked.

"So sorry, all my fault," Mr. Moon said, rushing over to her. "Are you okay? I must have gotten the snake spit and snail slime mixed up, you see, I…"

Mr. Goosepimple's eyebrows shot up. "That explains it," he said wearily.

"I thought *everyone* knew that putting together spider legs and snail slime causes explosions," said Bully Bogeywort scornfully, staring at Mr. Moon as if he were a particularly dense kind of troll.

Oliver glared at him, then at Casper, as the new boy snickered loudly.

"I'm terribly sorry," Mr. Moon said again, wringing his hands. He looked at Pippi. "Your poor hair! Shall I see if I can make you a Hair-conditioning potion, to grow that braid back?"

"No!" squealed Pippi, clapping her hands to her hair and stepping away from Mr. Moon.

"I could do it," drawled Casper, looking highly amused. "But I'd rather choose my own ingredients, thanks all the same."

"I've got some in my office you can use,

dear," Mrs. MacLizard told him, beckoning Pippi over. "Come along, Pippi. Thank you, Mr. Goosepimple. I hope the rest of the lesson is…*quieter* for you."

Casper snorted, then followed his aunt and Pippi out of the room.

Oliver watched them go, then glanced over at his dad, who was gingerly picking up Pippi's blackened beaker.

"Shall we try again?" Mr. Goosepimple said. He didn't sound very pleased, Oliver thought. "Mr. Moon, perhaps you could retrieve all the snail slime and give the students snake spit, as instructed. Then we might be able to get somewhere!"

"Yes, Mr. Goosepimple, of course, Mr. Goosepimple," Oliver's dad said, wiping his sooty hands on his overalls. "Snake spit coming right up. Um…whereabouts is it again?"

"Never mind," Mrs. Moon comforted her husband later that evening. The Witch Baby had just gone to bed, and Oliver and his parents were in the living room. "Everyone makes mistakes on their first day. Remember when I used to work at the Spell Supplies shop in town, and I turned my boss into a dragon's egg, on *my* first day?"

"And Pippi's braid *did* grow back again with the hair restorer…well, kind of," Oliver said, trying to be encouraging. "It's not quite the same color as the rest of her hair, but…"

Mr. Moon nodded. "I suppose you're right," he said. "I'm sure tomorrow will be better. I just need a little practice, that's all. Hadn't realized quite how rusty I'd gotten."

"Oh, you'll pick it up soon, I'm sure," Mrs. Moon said confidently.

Oliver grimaced as he remembered the look on Mrs. MacLizard's face in the Potions lab that afternoon. He really hoped his dad had a better day at Magic School tomorrow — for everyone's sake. He didn't want Bully *or* Casper to have anything to tease him about!

Chapter
Four

Over the next couple of days, Oliver got
to know Casper a little better – and his
first impressions weren't good. Casper was
a brilliant wizard, but such a show-off
with it!

When Casper was casting an
Obedience Charm over some wooly
spiders, they didn't just stay still to listen,

they actually sat down on their back four legs to pay full attention to him. With a smug smile on his face, Casper called the whole class over to watch as he commanded his spiders to balance in a tall, spindly-legged tower.

Oliver, whose own spiders seemed more interested in spinning webs down the table leg, could hardly bear to look.

On the next day, when Casper used the Transforma spell to turn grains of rice into giant headlice, he cast the spell so perfectly that the headlice all lined up neatly on Casper's desk, before leaping one by one into Nina Nettlewick's pigtails.

Oliver's giant headlice, on the other hand, were *too* giant. He had to cast a quick Stun spell to stop them before they made a break for anyone's hair and took an ear off with their great jaws.

If the new boy was showing his brilliance, the new Potions assistant was doing just the opposite. Poor Mr. Moon wasn't doing at all well in his new job. On Tuesday, he sent half the Year Fours home with food poisoning, after he spilled a jar of tox-beetles into a Full-belly potion they were making.

And on Wednesday, he got eagle feathers

confused with seagull feathers when the
Year Twelves were making Flying potions.
Once they'd drunk their potions, the Year
Twelves were transformed into seagulls
and flew miles to the coast to catch fish.

Mrs. MacLizard had to conjure up a special Summoning spell to get them all back to Cacklewick.

"He's such a birdbrain," Bully Bogeywort had sneered that afternoon. "Mr. Moon? Mr. Buffoon, more like!"

"Watch it!" Oliver had snapped hotly. "That's my dad you're talking about."

Casper had joined in. "So you must be Oliver Buffoon, then," he'd snickered. "Right?"

"Wrong," Oliver had growled. "And my dad's not a buffoon. He's just started his job, so give him a chance."

"Maybe I should ask my Aunty Madge to give him a chance," Casper had replied smartly. "A chance to get a new job!"

*

On Thursday afternoon, Mr. Moon got slightly mixed up when making a potion for the Year Ten Predictions lesson. Mr. Swish, the teacher, had asked for a "See" potion to help his class see into the future. Unfortunately, Mr. Moon had misunderstood, and had put together a "Sea" potion…which caused a flood of seawater to rush through the building.

It took Mrs. MacLizard half an hour to dry the floors with a Hot-air spell.

Of course, as Oliver and his classmates were outside, playing Wizardball, they got to see the torrents of water that came pouring out of the school. And it didn't take them long to find out who had caused it. Bully Bogeywort laughed so hard, he almost fell over.

"He's a disaster, that man. A total disaster!" Bully Bogeywort guffawed. "A zombie would do a better job!"

"Lay off, Bogey-brain," Oliver snapped. "Leave him alone. Everyone makes mistakes."

Bully Bogeywort fixed Oliver with his mean yellow eyes. "That's true, Oliver. And I'm looking at his *biggest* mistake right now – you."

"Oh, go away," Oliver said. "Go and fall off your broomstick somewhere painful."

"Ignore him, Ol," Jake said, bouncing his ball. "He's just jealous, because he knows you're the best wizard in the class. Come on, let's practice a few hoops."

"What? Oliver Buffoon, the best wizard in the class?" Bully Bogeywort replied, his eyes flicking across the Wizardball court to where Casper was shooting perfect practice goals one after another. "No chance. Not while Casper's here."

"Oliver's just as good a wizard as Casper is!" Jake retorted.

"Oh yeah?" Bully Bogeywort sneered, stalking away. "We'll see."

Oliver and Jake began passing the ball back and forth, taking turns throwing it through the Wizardball ring.

When everyone had warmed up, Ms. Smokeweaver, the Wizardball coach, split them into teams for a match. Casper was captain of the purple team, and Oliver was captain of the yellow team. Just as Ms. Smokeweaver blew her whistle to end the match, Casper scored the winning goal. "Well done, Purples – ten-nine, an amazing victory!" she cried. "Now off you go to get changed, everyone, it's time to go home."

Oliver felt crushed as he and Jake put on their school cloaks and set off for home. He was sick of Casper being so good at everything all the time. Just as

he was about to say as much to Jake,
a messenger sprite appeared in a thick
cloud of green smoke.

"Message!" the sprite trilled. "Oliver
Moon – your dad's a loser, and so are
you. I challenge you to a spell-off. Four
spells and a potion tomorrow
after school. From Casper!"

"What?" Oliver asked, blinking as the smoke swirled around his face. "A loser? A spell-off?"

"That's what I just said," the sprite replied, bowing deeply. "Magic competition, ain't it? Best wizard wins. Laters!"

The sprite vanished without another word. "Of all the nerve!" Oliver muttered crossly. "Who does that Casper think he is?"

"He's not messing around, is he?" Jake replied. "Four spells and a potion. Man. Serious stuff."

"Here he comes now," Oliver said, as they headed down toward the school driveway. Students were pouring down it, some on broomsticks, some walking —

and there was Casper striding up behind
Oliver and Jake. His cape swished along
behind him, like big black wings. As
Casper came closer, Oliver saw that the
new boy's eyes looked cold and hard.

"So, you think you're better than me, do you?" Casper said fiercely. "Think you can beat me in a spell-off?"

Oliver stared at him in disbelief. What nerve he had, coming to Magic School and picking fights like that! Why did he have it in for Oliver, anyway?

A hot feeling of rage surged through him. Well, he'd show Casper! "Yeah," he replied. "I do. And if I win, then you've got to promise never to say another mean word about me or my dad, okay?"

Casper laughed. "No problem," he replied confidently. He folded his arms in front of him. "And if *I* win – *when* I win, rather – you've got to quit talking about my Aunty Madge."

"What?" Oliver asked, feeling

bewildered. What did Mrs. MacLizard have to do with anything? "I never—"

Casper hadn't finished. "And to make it more interesting, let's throw in a little forfeit for the loser, too," he added, glaring.

"Fine," Oliver snapped. Then he wondered what he was getting himself into. But he couldn't back down now! "What sort of a forfeit?" he asked.

Casper thought for a moment. "Whoever loses the spell-off," he said slowly, "has to fly up to the highest school tower, and ride their broomstick all the way around it… blindfolded!"

Oliver gulped as he stared up at the tallest school tower. It was very, very high indeed. In fact, on a cloudy day, you couldn't even see the top of it!

"I don't think that's such a good idea," Jake said.

Casper leaned forward, a scornful look on his face. "Not…scared, are you, Oliver?" he asked.

Oliver shook his head. "No way," he fibbed. He held out his hand. "It's a deal," he said. "After school tomorrow."

Casper grabbed Oliver's hand and shook it hard, squeezing Oliver's fingers together. "Looking forward to it," he said.

Chapter Five

"I'll show him," Oliver said through gritted teeth as Casper marched away, nose in the air.

"Will you?" Jake asked doubtfully.

Oliver's shoulders slumped, and he couldn't help a little sigh. "Well...I hope so," he said. He stared after the new boy as he stalked off into the distance. "What did Casper mean, do you think, when he said he wanted me to stop talking about Mrs. MacLizard?"

Jake shook his head. "No idea. What have you been saying about her?"

"Nothing!" Oliver protested. "I can't *think* of anything I might have said, anyway." He couldn't help staring up at the top tower again. It looked even higher than it had two minutes ago. He really, *really* didn't want to fly all the way up there on his broomstick. He *had* to beat Casper in the spell-off. He just had to!

That night, Oliver got down to some serious studying. Four spells and a potion, the messenger sprite had said. That meant he and Casper would be choosing two spells each to challenge one another with. So Oliver had to come up with two difficult ones, which he'd be able to do but hopefully Casper couldn't, as well as prepare for whatever the new boy might throw at him. Knowing Casper, he'd probably pick some really obscure ones that Oliver had never even heard of.

Oliver worked hard all evening, until the Midnight Moon shone through his bedroom window, and his mom came and told him to turn the lamp off and go to bed. He fell asleep whispering spells to himself, and crossing all of his fingers.

When Oliver walked into the classroom the next morning at school, Casper was poring over a heavy spell book, nodding to himself in a pleased manner. He looked up and saw Oliver, then tapped a finger on the page he'd been reading and smirked. "This is going to separate the wizard from the wannabe," he said loudly. "You just wait, Oliver Moon."

Oliver sat down, feeling tense. Bully

Bogeywort caught his eye and winked. "I've been hearing all about this little spell-off. Can I watch?" he asked loudly.

"No way," Oliver said. It was bad enough doing the spell-off in the first place, but it would be even worse with Bully Bogeywort hanging around making rude comments.

"We *do* need a judge," Casper put in, overhearing.

"Yeah, but not *him*," Oliver said.

"I'll do it," Jake offered.

Casper narrowed his eyes. "But you're Oliver's friend! A judge isn't supposed to take sides," he pointed out.

"I won't!" Jake protested. "I'll—"

But Casper was already asking Colin Cockroach if he'd do it. "Sure," Colin said. "Loser flies around the tall tower, did you say? This I've got to see!"

Oliver felt sick all day. He could hardly concentrate in Cauldron Cooking Class. He couldn't sit still in Sorcery. And he fidgeted all the way through Fairy

Physics. After school had finished, Oliver, Jake, Casper and Colin walked along to the Potions room. Oliver's heart was pounding. His hands felt clammy. He really, really wished he could go home like everyone else right now.

Once in the Potions room, Colin fished in his cloak pocket for a coin, flipped it up in the air and slapped it down on his hand. "Oliver – hat or broomstick?"

"Hat," Oliver replied.

Colin uncovered the coin and they all bent over it. A broomstick was clearly visible on the silver coin. "Casper goes first," he declared solemnly.

Casper and Oliver walked to opposite ends of the room. Casper gave Oliver another of his frosty looks. "The first spell is…to conjure up a sky-dragon!" he called out.

Oliver's mind went blank. A sky-dragon? Oh, no! That was a really hard spell. He racked his brains, then waved his wand, chanting the words of the spell as they came to him. *"Lizard's leg and beetle's eye,"* he began hesitantly – then smiled in relief as he suddenly remembered the rest. *"I call a dragon to the sky!"*

There was a shower of silver sparks from his wand, and then a red dragon appeared in front of Oliver. It hovered in midair, flicking its scaly tail.

On the other side of the room, Casper's spell seemed to have worked perfectly too,

as a huge golden dragon had appeared.
It charged at the red dragon and
breathed fire on it. With a screech of fear,
the red dragon disappeared.

"One-nothing to Casper," Colin said,
backing away.

Casper smiled and clapped his hands. The golden dragon turned into thousands of tiny golden sparkles, then vanished completely.

Oliver gripped his wand, his mouth dry. Now it was his turn. He really hoped Casper would struggle with *this* one. "The second spell is to…turn yourself invisible!" he shouted.

He waved his wand, and chanted the spell: "*Make me not there, turn me to…*"

Oliver started coughing. His mouth was so dry, he could hardly get the last word out. "*Air!*" he croaked hoarsely.

Across the other side of the room, he could see that Casper had completely disappeared. Rats!

He looked down at himself. His left

foot was still clearly visible for all to see. Double rats!

"Sorry, Ol," Jake said. "I can still see you."

"It's two-nothing to Casper!" Colin announced.

Casper appeared again, grinning. "I'm enjoying this," he said. "Spell number three. Oh, and if I beat you on this one, then I've won, right? Better get that blindfold ready, Oliver!"

Oliver wiped his sweaty hands on his cloak. "Get on with it," he muttered.

"Spell number three," Casper said. "Make yourself fly!"

Oliver thought back to his dad's eagle/seagull disaster as he raised his wand, ready to wave it. But before he could open his mouth, Casper had already chanted a spell and he rose off the ground triumphantly, flapping his arms and sticking out his tongue.

A brilliant idea struck Oliver then, and he waved his wand over himself. Everyone knew that eagles could fly higher than wizards, didn't they? Maybe if he went one better than a simple flying command, he could beat Casper this time!

"Wing and claw and beady eye.

Let me fly like eagles fly!" he shouted.

Instantly, feathers began sprouting all over his body, and his arms became wings. Oliver laughed out loud as he flapped them hard and soared effortlessly off the ground, leaving Casper far below.

Jake let out a cheer. "Surely Oliver wins that one?"

Colin nodded. "Oliver pulls one back. It's two-one to Casper!"

Casper scowled. "When I said flying, I meant as a wizard," he said, landing on the ground once more with a thump.

Oliver did a loop the loop over the ingredients cabinet. "Can't hear you, sorry," he called. "I'm too high up!"

Once Oliver had landed and turned back into his usual self, he took a deep breath. His turn now, and the next spell he'd chosen was a difficult one. If Casper messed it up, Oliver could even the score up to two-all. "Spell number four — become a lion!" he shouted.

He waved his wand for a fourth time, chanting the spell as he did so.

"Mane and tail,
Growl and claw,
This lion has a powerful ROAR!"

He felt his body expanding, and then fur began sprouting all over him. He dropped down on all fours, swishing his tail and growling.

The same thing happened to Casper, and within moments there were two lions baring their teeth at each other across the lab.

Colin stepped between them and eyed them cautiously. "No fighting, no biting, judge's rules," he said, with a nervous catch in his voice. He looked from one

lion to the other. "Hmmm. Both excellent. Too close to call," he decided. "This one's a draw! Score stays at two-one to Casper."

Oliver roared in disappointment as he turned back into a boy once more. He'd really thought he was going to get that point, too! Which meant that as the score stood, he just *had* to win the last round. Otherwise...

Oliver gulped. Otherwise Casper would have won the spell-off and he, Oliver, would be flying around the top tower, blindfolded!

Chapter
Six

"The final round is the Potions test," Colin said. "To make things fair, I'm going to flick through the Potions book and open it at random, okay?"

Casper and Oliver both nodded, and Colin shut his eyes and ran a thumb down the pages of the big black Potions book that lived in the lab. "This one!"

he declared, opening it halfway through.

The Potions book gave a chuckle. "He's picked a good 'un!" it said in a breathy, rustling sort of a voice. "The Hooting potion! Get it right, and  you'll hoot like an owl. Get it wrong, and you'll squawk like a parrot."

Oliver couldn't help a nervous flinch. He'd never tried the Hooting potion before. He scanned the ingredients list quickly, as did Casper. A dozen hairy caterpillars, three feathers from an owl, a slither of toadspawn...

"Collect your ingredients...now!" Jake called.

Oliver and Casper rushed down to the

Potions cabinet, and grabbed a beaker
each. With trembling fingers, Oliver
counted out twelve hairy caterpillars,
and then three white owl feathers.
Casper did the same.

And then, just as they reached for the toadspawn jar, Oliver saw a label on it, in his dad's handwriting. The frogspawn jar also had a label with Mr. Moon's loopy handwriting. And Oliver hesitated. He knew very well that his dad always, *always* got frogspawn and toadspawn mixed up. That meant the jar that read "toadspawn" would really have frogspawn in it. And the jar labeled "frogspawn" was sure to have toadspawn in it.

Casper opened the jar marked "toadspawn" and scooped some out into his jar. "That's me done," he announced, pushing past Oliver to get to his desk.

While Casper started on his potion, Oliver took the jar marked "frogspawn"

and spooned out a dollop. It was a
gamble, he knew. But he had to give it
a try.

The two boys worked in silence,
grinding and heating and mixing, until
they both had a potion ready. Casper's
was bright green. Oliver's was yellow.

"Interesting," Casper said, raising his eyebrows. "After three? One, two, three... DRINK!"

Both boys lifted their beakers to their mouths and then, crossing his fingers with his free hand, Oliver took a big mouthful and swallowed it down.

Ugh! It tasted absolutely vile. "Too-whit-too-whoo!" he hooted in disgust. And then his mouth fell open in delight. He'd hooted! He'd gotten it right! And it was all thanks to his dad, getting it *wrong*!

Casper let out a squawk…and his face fell. His Hooting potion hadn't worked. He sounded like a parrot.

"Oliver gets a point, so you both finish up with two points each!" Colin announced, and laughed. "It's a draw! So that means Casper, you can't be mean about Oliver's dad anymore, and Oliver…" He hesitated. "What was your side of the deal, Casper?"

The potions were wearing off. Casper squawked a few times and then replied. "Oliver can't say anything else horrible about my Aunty Madge," he said firmly.

"Too-whit-too-*what?*" Oliver asked. "I never said anything horrible about her in the first place! I *like* Mrs. MacLizard!"

Casper looked at him suspiciously. "What about that magic message you sent me, then? Where you said I was an egghead and my aunt was a warty walrus?"

"A warty walrus?" echoed Oliver in shock. "I didn't say that! And I didn't call you an egghead either!" He stared at Casper. "You were the one who started the name-calling. What was it you said? That my dad was a loser, and so was I!"

Casper shook his head slowly. "I didn't say any of that," he told Oliver. He narrowed his eyes, thinking. "And I didn't challenge you to this spell-off either."

Oliver gulped. "You didn't? Well, it wasn't *my* idea. So who...?"

The thought struck them at exactly the same time. "Bully Bogeywort," Oliver groaned.

"He set us up!" Casper exclaimed. "The messages were both from him!"

"The double-crossing toad!" Colin gasped.

"Of all the sneaky…" Jake spluttered, shaking his head.

Casper looked thoughtful. "There must be a way we can get back at him," he said. "We can't let him get away with this, Oliver!"

Oliver nodded. "You're right," he said. "Let me think…"

The boys left the Potions room and started walking down the corridor. "We could put a Hairless hex on him," Casper said with a grin. "He'll be bald as a beetle by breakfast."

Oliver spluttered with laughter. "Or we could put a Tight-hat curse on him, so that his pointy hat sticks to his head all day and night," he suggested.

"Hey, look, there he is," Jake said, pointing as Bully Bogeywort stomped out of the main school doors, his

broomstick under his arm. "How come he's leaving school so late today?"

"Detention with Mrs. MacLizard for getting caught skipping Broomstick Training," Colin told them.

They followed Bully out and watched as he swung a leg over his broomstick and prepared to fly off home.

Oliver's eyes gleamed, and he turned to Casper. "I've got an idea," he said. "Maybe since neither of *us* got to fly around the tallest tower, we should let Bully have the pleasure…"

"Yes!" Casper laughed. "Perfect, Oliver!" He raised his wand with a grin. "You do a Blindfolding spell, and I'll hex his broomstick. Ready…set…GO!"

The two boys pointed their wands at

Bully Bogeywort and muttered a series of magic words each. Then they all watched as a large pink blindfold appeared from out of nowhere on Bully's face, covering his eyes. In the same moment, his broomstick started jiggling impatiently beneath him.

"Hey!" they heard him cry, trying to rip off the blindfold. "What's this? What's going on?"

"Hold on tight and enjoy the ride, Bully!" Casper shouted out.

"Have fun!" bellowed Oliver.

Then they all stood and watched the extraordinary sight of Bully Bogeywort's broomstick dragging him around and around the tallest tower of the school, while its rider shouted and squealed in fright.

Oliver couldn't stop laughing —
especially when Bully Bogeywort landed
in a huge muddy puddle.

"Priceless," Oliver said, wiping the
tears from his eyes as he watched Bully
wrench off the pink blindfold and look
around in a daze.

Casper turned to Oliver. "I reckon
that was almost worth having to do the
spell-off!" he said.

Oliver grinned. "Definitely," he said.
"We make a good team! All four of us."

Oliver high-fived his friends, and they
headed home for dinner.

The End

Oliver Moon, Junior Wizard

Join Oliver and his friends
for more magical mayhem at

www.olivermoon.com

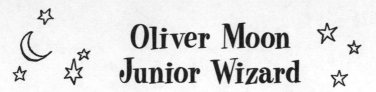

Oliver Moon
Junior Wizard

Collect all of Oliver Moon's magical adventures!

Oliver Moon and the Potion Commotion
Can Oliver create a potion to win the Young Wizard of the Year award?

Oliver Moon and the Dragon Disaster
Oliver's sure his new pet dragon will liven up the Festival of Magic...

Oliver Moon and the Nipperbat Nightmare
Things go horribly wrong when Oliver gets to look after the school pet.

Oliver Moon's Summer Howliday
Oliver suspects there is something odd about his hairy new friend, Wilf.

Oliver Moon's Christmas Cracker
Can a special present save Oliver's Christmas at horrible Aunt Wart's?

Oliver Moon and the Spell-off
Oliver must win a spell-off against clever Casper to avoid a scary forfeit.

Oliver Moon's Fangtastic Sleepover
Will Oliver survive a school sleepover in the haunted house museum?

Oliver Moon and the Broomstick Battle
Can Oliver beat Bully to win the Junior Wizards' Obstacle Race?

Happy Birthday, Oliver Moon
Will Oliver's birthday party be ruined when his invitations go astray?

Oliver Moon and the Spider Spell
Oliver's Grow-bigger spell lands the Witch Baby's pet in huge trouble.

Oliver Moon and the Troll Trouble
Can Oliver save the show as the scary, stinky troll in the school play?

Oliver Moon and the Monster Mystery
Strange things start to happen when Oliver wins a monster raffle prize...